For Michael, Alessia, Thomas, Fido, Number 1, and Number 2, with love
—ST

For my grandmother, Mombo
—CL

Library of Congress Cataloging-in-Publication data is on file with the publisher.

First published in the United States of America in 2019 by Albert Whitman & Company
ISBN 978-0-8075-7730-1

Printed in China
10 9 8 7 6 5 4 3 2 1 WKT 22 21 20 19 18

Design by Rick DeMonico

For more information about Albert Whitman & Company,
visit our website at www.albertwhitman.com.

100 Years of Albert Whitman & Company
Celebrate with us in 2019!

Taking a Walk
Spring in the Woods

Sue Tarsky

illustrated by
Claire Lordon

Albert Whitman & Company
Chicago, Illinois

I went for a walk in the woods today.
I saw lots of trees.

Some of them looked like lollipops!

I went for a walk in the woods today.
I saw green trees and one brown bear.

The brown bear was very big!

I went for a walk in the woods today.
I saw green trees, one big brown bear,
and two blue birds.

The birds sang a song for me!

I went for a walk in the woods today.

I saw green trees, one big brown bear, two blue birds,

and three bushy-tailed red foxes.

The foxes did not see me!

I went for a walk in the woods today.

I saw green trees, one big brown bear, two blue birds,

three bushy-tailed red foxes, and four brown deer.

The deer had great big antlers!

I went for a walk in the woods today.
I saw green trees, one big brown bear, two blue birds,
three bushy-tailed red foxes, four brown deer,
and five gray squirrels.

The squirrels were leaping from tree to tree!

I went for a walk in the woods today.

I saw green trees, one big brown bear, two blue birds,

three bushy-tailed red foxes, four brown deer,

five gray squirrels, and six pink flowers.

The flowers were blowing in the wind!

I went for a walk in the woods today.
I saw green trees, one big brown bear, two blue birds,
three bushy-tailed red foxes, four brown deer,
five gray squirrels, six pink flowers,
and seven yellow bumblebees.

The bumblebees were buzzing around the flowers!

I went for a walk in the woods today.

I saw green trees, one big brown bear, two blue birds,

three bushy-tailed red foxes, four brown deer,

five gray squirrels, six pink flowers,

seven yellow bumblebees, and eight orange caterpillars.

The caterpillars were crawling along the leaves!

I went for a walk in the woods today.
I saw green trees, one big brown bear, two blue birds,
three bushy-tailed red foxes, four brown deer,
five gray squirrels, six pink flowers,
seven yellow bumblebees, eight orange caterpillars,
and nine little white rabbits.

The rabbits saw me and hopped away!

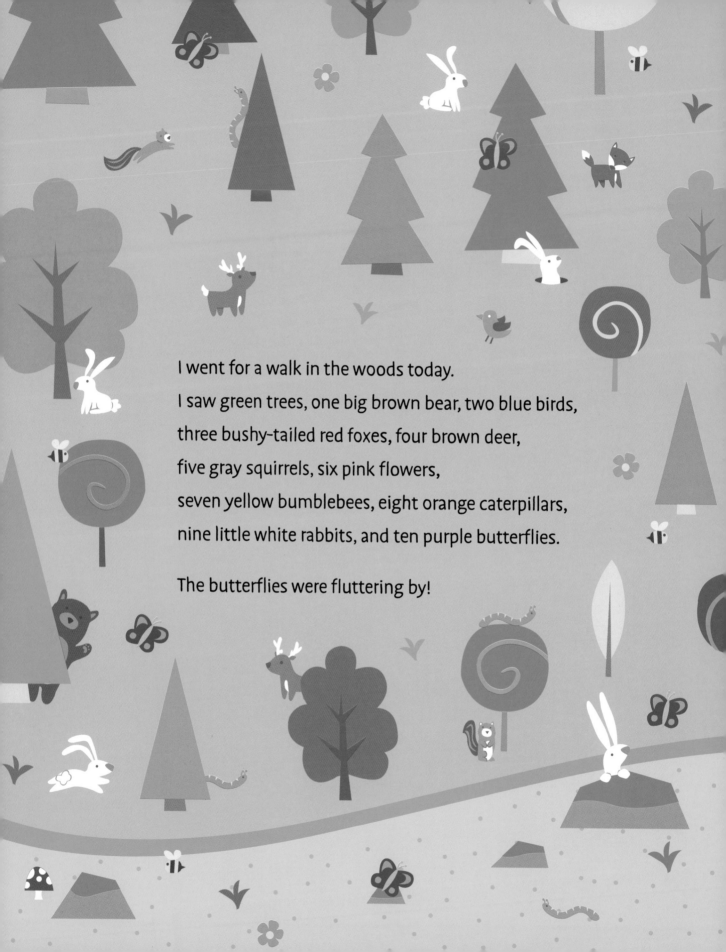

I went for a walk in the woods today.

I saw green trees, one big brown bear, two blue birds,

three bushy-tailed red foxes, four brown deer,

five gray squirrels, six pink flowers,

seven yellow bumblebees, eight orange caterpillars,

nine little white rabbits, and ten purple butterflies.

The butterflies were fluttering by!

I went for a walk in the woods today. I saw

lots of green trees

1 big brown bear

2 blue birds

3 bushy-tailed red foxes

4 brown deer

5 gray squirrels

6 pink flowers

7 yellow bumblebees

8 orange caterpillars

9 little white rabbits

and 10 purple butterflies.

What a good walk I had!

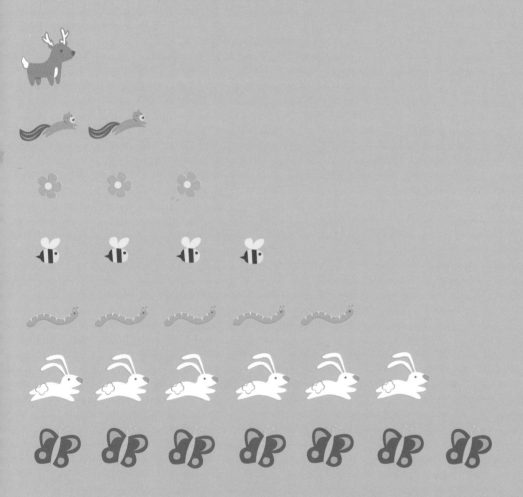

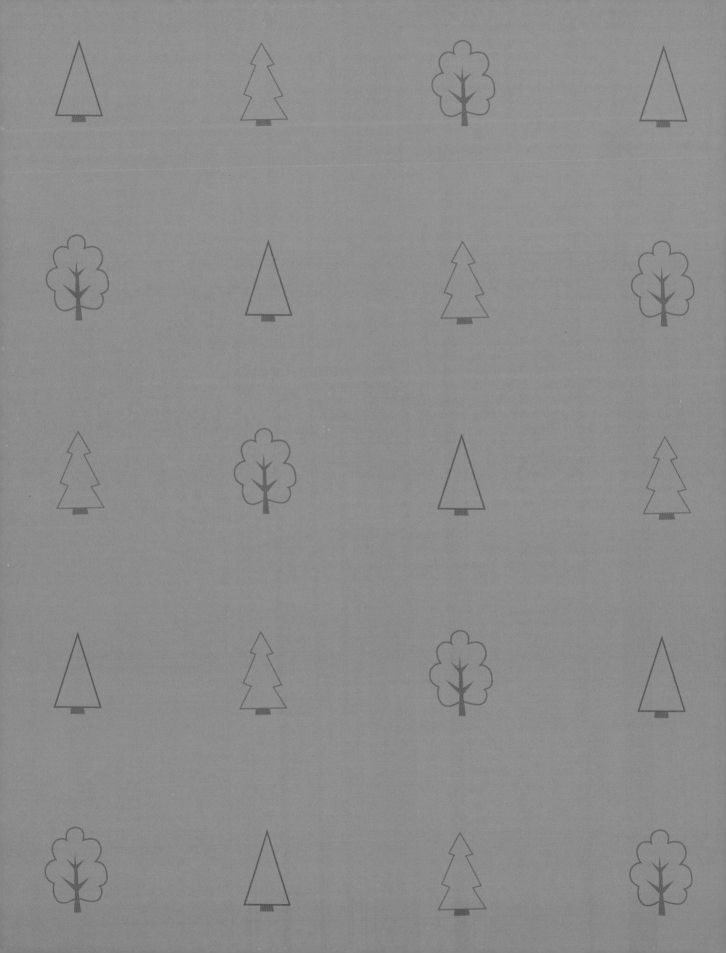